The Little Pen

D0864711

Tom loves going on beach holidays with his mum. Every year they do the same things. But this year is different. One night there is a huge storm and the next day the beach is covered in seaweed, and there, in the sand, Tom finds a tiny penguin, barely alive. How can he and Mum help?

Happy Cat First Readers

The Little Penguin

Raewyn Caisley

Illustrated by
Ann James

HAPPY CAT BOOKS

JS

Published by
Happy Cat Books
An imprint of Catnip Publishing Ltd
14 Greville Street
London EC1N 8SB

First published by Penguin Books, Australia, 2006

This edition first published 2011
3 5 7 9 10 8 6 4 2

A CIP catalogue record for this book is available
from the British Library

ISBN: 978-1-905117-58-1

Printed in India

www.catnippublishing.co.uk

For *my* little buddy, Jack. *R.C.*

For Nikki, who's good at finding things and knowing what to do with them. *A.J.*

Acknowledgments

I'd like to acknowledge the work of the many volunteers who sit on beaches all over Australia caring for our native wildlife.

My thanks go to Barbara from Orca. *R.C.*

Chapter 1

Tom loved going on holiday
with Mum. They always
went to the same place, a
little beach way up north.
He'd spend half the trip
curled up on pillows in
the back of the car. For
the rest of the time they'd

play 'I spy' until finally
the caravan park came
in sight.

Every year they stayed
in the same rickety old
caravan. It was in the
furthest corner of the
caravan park, next to the
beach. It had a little path
made of broken shells that
crunched under Tom's feet
as he carried the bags
inside.

Once they'd unpacked
they'd go and get fish
and chips for tea from
Mr Guthrie's shop.

'Goodness me, you've
grown,' Mr Guthrie would
say.

He'd sprinkle their tea
with salt and vinegar and
Tom would carry the hot
parcel home under his
shirt. It left a red patch on
his chest.

Before bed, Tom and Mum would go for a walk on the beach.

They'd watch the sun go down and Mum would try to work out what the weather would be like the next day.

Last year she'd said, 'Fishing weather tomorrow, Tom!' He couldn't figure out how she knew.

This year even he could

see what was coming.
Clouds boiled like porridge
in a pot and lightning cut
into the sea.

'Better batten down the
hatches tonight,' Mum said.

Tom thought about being
tucked up, safe and warm,
with the storm bumping
into the caravan, and Mum
asleep in the fold-down bed.

Chapter 2

While Mum and Tom slept,
a battle raged over the
ocean. The wind blew up
waves the size of cargo
ships, and clouds hugged
the earth, blocking out
the moon and stars. The
sea rolled and shifted,

tumbling tiny things about.

In the morning they
woke to rain washing over
the caravan. They played
games inside all day until,

late in the afternoon, Mum
said, 'Let's go and see what
the storm's thrown up.'

Tom ran ahead of Mum.
He turned into the track

that led to the sand-dunes. Pumping his legs, he climbed to the top.

Beneath him the beach was covered with an enormous serve of seaweed. It looked like cabbage on a plate.

The waves had carved a little cliff near the water's edge. Tom ran towards it, but just as he was about to jump off,

he saw something in the
sand below.

He stopped and looked
to see what the storm had
sent him.

A penguin lay at his feet,
its flippers stretched out
flat as if it were dead.

Chapter 3

Tom jumped down off the
little cliff. He reached out
and touched the penguin's
feathers. They were crisp
and spiky, like dog hair.

He dropped to his knees
and wiped his hands on his
pants. Very carefully he

cupped his hands around
the penguin. It was like his
football, round and hard.
He could feel the beating of
its heart.

Bump, bump. Bump,
bump. Bump, bump.

He smiled.

'What have you got
there?' Mum asked as he
came climbing back up the
dunes. She'd been watching
from the look-out bench.

Very quietly Tom said,
'It's a penguin.'

He held it out for Mum
to take.

Flap, flap. Flap, flap. The
penguin sprayed them both
with salt and sand and
seawater.

'We need a box,' said
Mum. 'I don't think he likes
us holding him.'

Tom ran back to the
caravan. He emptied out

their box of groceries. Then he took the fish-and-chip paper out of the sink and put it in the box.

Tom knew that penguins ate fish. He hoped the penguin would like the fishy smell.

Mum came up the caravan steps.

'That looks comfortable,' she said, and she carefully put the penguin in.

Crunch, crunch, flap, flap,
crunch, crunch, it went,
struggling in its paper bed.

'What do we do with him now?' Tom asked.

'I'm not sure,' Mum said, gently stroking the

penguin's head. 'Perhaps
we should get some expert
help.'

Chapter 4

Tom carried the box down
to Mr Guthrie's shop. He
had his arms underneath
so that the bottom wouldn't
fall out. He waited outside
while Mum went in to buy
a phone card. The penguin
opened its beak a tiny bit,

but that was all.

'I wish he'd close his beak,' Tom said when Mum came back with the card.

'Just let him lie there quietly,' said Mum.

Mum phoned some people who knew all about penguins.

'They say penguins can get lost quite easily,' she said after she hung up.

'Sometimes they have trouble finding food, and sometimes they find playmates and stay out in the water too long, but they think our one just got caught in the storm.'

'I don't think he likes it in the box,' said Tom.

'No,' agreed Mum. Then she said, 'We shouldn't have picked him up. He might

be suffering from shock.
We have to take him back
to the beach.'

Tom looked at Mum.

'I'm sorry,' he said, and
his eyes filled up with
tears. 'I didn't mean to
hurt him.'

Mum gave him a hug and
said, 'I know.'

They both looked into
the box.

'They're sending someone

to look after him,' said
Mum. 'How about taking
him home?'

Chapter 5

The penguin gave one weak flap as they walked back to the sand-dunes, and then it lay quiet and still. Tom didn't really want to carry it any more but he didn't say so.

He swallowed hard.

'Where was he again?'
Mum asked.

Tom nodded towards the
little cliff.

'Let's wait here for a
while,' said Mum, and they

sat down on the look-out
bench.

A lady wearing a whale
T-shirt arrived. She came

puffing up the dunes,
carrying a thermos and
a bright blue bag. Her hair
was long like a mermaid's
hair and she had dolphin
earrings. She sat beside
Mum and Tom.

'Aren't you good,' she said,
looking into the box. 'If only
everyone cared so much.'

She stroked Tom's hair.

'I'm Alice,' she said, and
then she asked, 'Do you

know a safe place where we could leave him, Tom? Somewhere away from dogs.'

Tom remembered a little cave where he'd left his yellow digger once.

The whale lady smiled and said, 'That sounds perfect.'

Chapter 6

Together they went to find the cave. Their shadows were getting long and thin, and the sea was flat and grey. The whale lady looked at Tom.

'Did Mum tell you he might die?' she asked.

Tom felt his heart being squashed as if someone was holding it in their hands.

'He's a wild animal, you see,' she said.

'But I was careful,' Tom whispered. His voice could hardly find its way out.

'Of course you were,' the whale lady said. 'But he might be sick inside. We'll put him in your cave tonight and I'll stay with him for a while. You never know. He might just have a little sleep and then decide to swim back out to sea.'

Silently they walked past the mountains of seaweed. When they reached the cave, Tom put the box down.

'Would you like me to lift him out?' the whale lady asked.

Tom shook his head.
Carefully he cupped his
hands around the penguin.

Now it felt like his football
when it needed pumping
up. The penguin's flippers
hung down, limp and soft.
He laid it on the floor of
the cave.

Suddenly the little
penguin's eyelids fluttered.
It opened its beak wide and
then closed it again.

'You go to sleep now,' Tom
whispered.

They sat outside the cave

for half an hour. The whale
lady gave Tom a muesli bar.
He lay on his stomach and
watched the penguin. Its
eyes were shut so tight it
seemed to frown.

'Come on, Tom,' Mum
said at last. 'We'd better go
and make tea.'

'But I don't want to go,'
said Tom.

The whale lady smiled at
Tom again.

'Don't worry,' she said,

'I'll look after him.'

Chapter 7

Mum and Tom went to buy some bread. Mr Guthrie handed Tom the bag.

'I hear you two have rescued a little penguin,' he said.

'We took him back to the beach,' said Tom.

'Best place for him,'
Mr Guthrie agreed. 'Don't
worry. If Alice is on the job,
she'll do everything she can.'

Back at the caravan
Mum put baked beans in a
pot.

Tom usually loved the
smell of the cooking gas,

and after fish and chips, baked beans were his favourite. But it didn't matter tonight.

He put on his rocket pyjamas and brushed his teeth. Then he and Mum went to use the toilet block. Tom could smell the sea as they walked along.

'Can we go and have another look?' he asked.

Mum nodded.

It was getting dark now.
When they reached
the top of the dunes Tom
climbed onto the look-out

bench. A light twinkled
down by the cave.

'Looks like Alice is doing
a good job,' said Mum.

'Come on, little buddy, time for bed.'

Mum brushed the sand off Tom's feet before tucking him in.

'Can we go back in the morning?' he asked.

'Of course we can,' said Mum, and she gave him a goodnight kiss.

Tom woke up half way through the night. He felt cold. He pulled his blankets

up and wondered if it was
cold in the cave.

'I'm sure he'll be all
right,' whispered Mum.

Tom lifted the curtain
above his bed, but he
couldn't see anything
except the moon.

Chapter 8

In the morning Tom ran down to the beach in his pyjamas. He reached the top of the dunes and looked everywhere but he couldn't see anyone.

His heart jumped up to the top of his throat.

He ran down the other side, trying not to think about what might have happened. Sand stung his face.

Outside the cave, he dropped to his knees. There was a funny little football shape in the sand, some stones and a bit of dried seaweed, but apart from that the penguin's cave was empty.

'Oh,' said Tom.

He wiped a sandy hand across his face.

All of a sudden Mum was sitting beside him. 'Shall we go and get some breakfast?' she said.

She stood up and held her hand out.

Tiny waves tumbled onto the beach as they walked home. Tom imagined the smell of toast in the caravan.

'Did he swim back out to sea?' he asked.

Mum squeezed his hand.

'Yes. I'm sure he did,' she said.

From Raewyn Caisley

The caravan bits in my story are straight from my own childhood holidays . . . the cooking gas smell, the sound of rain on the caravan roof, having baked beans and fish and chips, running down to the beach after a storm.

I once found a little penguin washed up on the beach. Like Mum and Tom, I didn't know what to do with him. I put him in a cave, but he was just too worn out and died in the night. I hope Tom's penguin survived.

From Ann James

I am very good at finding things,
partly because I'm very interested
in looking for things. Sometimes
I go with my nephew Daniel and
his sisters Andie and Nikki for long
walks along the canal behind their
home. It's shallow and narrow and
we can jump across it easily. Along
the way we look for treasures. Now
and again I have found a living
treasure, like Tom did.

The Princess and the Unicorn

Wendy Blaxland

No one believes in unicorns any more. Except Princess Lily, that is.
So when the king falls ill and the only thing that can cure him is
the magic of a unicorn, it's up to her to find one.
But can Lily find a magical unicorn in time?

Becky was cross with her little brother. 'If you don't leave me alone,' she said to him, 'I'll put a spell on you!' But she didn't mean to make him disappear!

Crystal longs to be a mermaid.
Her mother makes her a flashing silver tail. But it isn't like
being a proper mermaid. Then one night Crystal wears her
tail to bed...

Jock can make a special sound like a duck!
If you can learn to make it too you can help Jock rescue the
little duck from the duck hunter. Quick, before it's too late!

David's had a party invitation!
It's a dressing-up party and he's going to go as a fox. But
when he arrives he can see he's made a mistake in choosing
his costume. Can he still fit in with the party theme and
have fun?

Nicholas Nosh is the littlest pirate in the world. He's not allowed
to go to sea. 'You're too small,' said his dad. But when the fierce
pirate Captain Red Beard kidnaps his family, Nicholas sets sail
to rescue them!

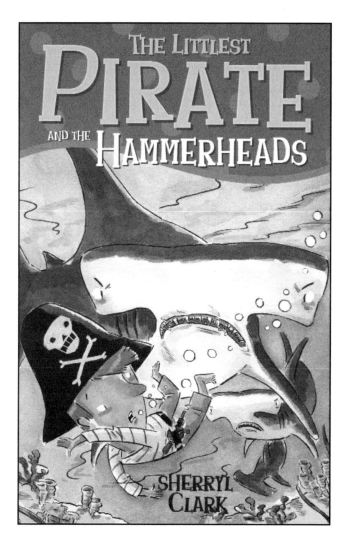

Nicholas Nosh, the littlest pirate in the world, has to rescue his family's treasure which has been stolen by Captain Hammerhead. But how can he outwit the sharks that are guarding Captain Hammerhead's ship?

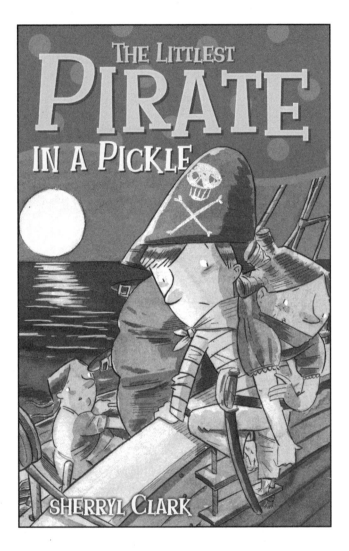

Nicholas Nosh is teased by his cousin Primrose for
being so small. But when Captain Manners of the
Jolly Dodger kidnaps her, Nicholas shows just how
brave a little pirate he can be!